The Pink House

Kate Salley Palmer

Published by Warbranch Press, Inc.,
329 Warbranch Rd., Central, SC 29630

Warbranch Press, Inc.

ISBN 0-9667114-1-6

Published by Warbranch Press, Inc.
329 Warbranch Road
Central, SC 29630

First Printing

Warbranch Press, Inc.

This book is for
All the aunts,
All the uncles,
All the cousins,
And even Grandma

Every summer, all the aunts, all the uncles, and even Grandma gather at the Pink House at Edisto Beach. We gather there, too! We are cousins! There are six of us--three little cousins, two big cousins, and one new baby cousin!

My cousins call my dad "Uncle James." When Dad comes to the Pink House, he brings his tools.

My cousins call my mom "Aunt Marty." When she comes to the Pink House, Mom brings one little cousin (me!) Mom also brings snacks, and a whole bag of books to share!

Aunt Margaret is my mom's sister. She doesn't bring any cousins to the Pink House...

...but sometimes she brings Uncle Pook! Aunt Margaret also brings lots of canned drinks and her tiny T.V. When Uncle Pook comes to the Pink House, he brings his easel and his brushes and his paints

Uncle Bill is my mom's brother. When he comes to the Pink House, Uncle Bill brings two little cousins and the new baby cousin!
He brings Aunt Jaymie, too. Aunt Jaymie brings a cake and games to play.

Aunt Kate is my mom's other sister. When she comes to the Pink House, Aunt Kate brings Uncle Jim and the two big cousins! Aunt Kate also brings her guitar and a big jar of spaghetti sauce.

Uncle Jim brings fishing rods and tackle boxes. When Grandma comes to the Pink House, she brings toys and surprises for everyone!

We help each other make beds.

The two big cousins like to sleep on the porch, where the nights blow cooler and the waves roll louder and the moon shines brighter. Lucky big cousins!

After we've unpacked our things at the Pink House,
all the aunts, all the uncles, all the cousins, and even
Grandma put on our bathing suits so we can go swimming.
We smear ourselves with lotion so we won't get a sunburn.
We wear our shoes so we won't get stickers in our feet.
(The big cousins sometimes forget to wear their shoes.)

We all go down the steps and through the sand to the ocean. Even the new baby cousin, who wears a teensy little bathing suit, a teensy little bit of suntan lotion, and teensy little shoes.

And even Uncle Pook, who wears his shoes everywhere anyway and never swims in the water or sits in the sun without a hat.

"Let's fish in the surf," say Uncle Jim and Uncle Bill. "With our nets and rods and reels! Maybe we can catch enough fish to have for supper!"

"you do that," say Aunt Jaymie, Aunt Marty, and Aunt Kate. "We'll read our books in the sunshine! Maybe we'll read all the books we brought!"

"Come on!" says Grandma, "We're going crabbing! First, we'll tie some smelly old chicken necks to a line for bait. (Crabs think smelly old chicken necks are delicious.) We'll put the line of bait into the water."

"When crabs come to take the food, we'll catch them in our long-handled nets! Maybe we'll catch enough for everyone to have crab cakes!"

After lunch at the Pink House, we have to take naps on the porch. Uncle Pook paints while We nap!

Now the screen door is fixed, but we need to cool off! The two big cousins take us to the water. We swim in the surf and let the waves splash all around us!

We get out of the water to help Aunt Margaret search for petrified shark's teeth on the beach. They're hard to find, but they're very pretty—all sharp and shiny-black. Maybe we'll find enough to make a necklace!

When the shadows grow long and the sun hangs over the
live oaks like an orange balloon...all the aunts, all the uncles,
all the cousins, and even Grandma go up to the Pink House
to take an outside shower to wash away the
sand and salt water and tiny seashells
that stick to our hair and bathing suits.

...All except Uncle Pook. He never gets sand, or salt water or seashells on himself in the first place.

All the clean little cousins, the clean big cousins, the clean aunts, and even clean Grandma sing songs on the deck while Aunt Kate plays the guitar. We take turns rocking the new baby cousin.

The kitchen gets very messy!

Uncle James, Uncle Jim, and Uncle Bill fry fish, shrimp, and hushpuppies for supper.

They bake crabcakes, too!

After supper, all the aunts, all the uncles, all the cousins, and even Grandma play games. Uncle Pook likes to call out the questions and keep score. The new baby cousin laughs at everything and then goes to sleep.

Then, all the aunts, all the uncles, all the cousins, and even Grandma snuggle into our Pink House beds and listen to the sound of the waves washing the beach smoothing the sand leaving surprises

for us to find in the morning.